Cassie the Cat

Pedro the Penguin

Zoe the Zebra

Sonia the
Snow Rabbit

Chesney the Cheetah

Paul the Python

First published in 2012 by Hodder Children's Books
Copyright © Get Well Friends Ltd.

WWW.GETWELLFRIENDS.COM

Hodder Children's Books, 338 Euston Road, London, NW1 3BH
Hodder Children's Books Australia, Level 17/207 Kent Street, Sydney, NSW 2000

The right of Kes Gray to be identified as the author and Mary McQuillan as the illustrator
of this Work has been asserted by them in accordance with the Copyright, Designs and Patents Act 1988.

A catalogue record of this book is available from the British Library.

ISBN: 978 1 444 90028 6

Hodder Children's Books is a division of Hachette Children's Books
An Hachette UK Company
www.hachette.co.uk

MOMO
goes Flying!

Kes Gray & Mary McQuillan

Hodder
Children's
Books

A division of Hachette Children's Books

Hello! I'm Nurse Nibbles,

and these are my get well friends.

In my hospital,
I have lots of comfy
chairs of ALL
shapes and sizes.

Which is a good job because poorly animals
come to visit me from ALL over the world!

I've looked after  beetles with back pain, horses with hayfever,

turtles with toothache,  moles with measles,  and even crayfish with cramp!

This morning a new poorly patient came to see me. His name was Momo the monkey and he had a very sore arm indeed!

This is the story of how Momo the monkey went flying...

One day, Momo the very cheeky monkey
was playing high up on the branch of
a mango tree.

Far below, on the rainforest floor, he saw a tiger washing his whiskers.

Momo smiled mischievously and picked a mango from the tree.

"OUCH!" said the tiger,
as the mango bounced off his head.
"Who did that?"

"TEE HEE!" giggled Momo, using the long green vines to escape through the trees.

Momo swung up into
another tree and
looked down again.

Far below, on the forest floor,
an elephant was dozing peacefully.

"YOUCH!"

said the elephant, as a whole bunch
of bananas bounced off her head.
"Who threw that?" she said,
peering up at the tree.

"You'll never know," chuckled Momo,
swinging from vine to vine in search of
more animals to play tricks on.

"OUCH!"
said a civet,
as berries
bounced off
her back.

"OUCH!" said a pig,
as lychees bounced
off her head.

"OUCH!" said a mongoose,
as nuts rained down onto
his shoulders.

"STOP RIGHT THERE!"

said the long green vine that
Momo had grabbed hold of.

Momo lurched forward in mid swing
and realised his mistake. It wasn't a long
green vine at all – it was the tail of...

...a long green SNAKE!

"Take that, you cheeky monkey!" said the snake,
wrapping its tail tightly around Momo's wrist
and catapulting him through the air.

"OUCH!"
whimpered Momo, crunching his arm into the trunk of a tree.

"OUCH!"
he groaned, tumbling to the forest floor below.

"OUCH,
OUCH,
OUCH!"
he said as an avalanche of mangoes clattered onto his head.

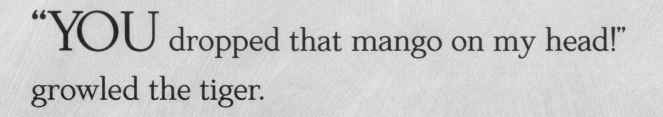

"YOU dropped that mango on my head!" growled the tiger.

"YOU threw those bananas!" trumpeted the elephant.

"And the lychees, the nuts and the berries!" frowned the other animals, who had gathered at the foot of the tree.

"My arm hurts!" moaned Momo, trying to raise his paw to say sorry. "It's been grabbed and yanked and rocketed and crunched!"

No wonder Momo's arm felt so sore!
Never mind, the good news is that when
Momo came to visit me, he was a very
well behaved monkey indeed.

He let me put a sling on his arm, and some ointment on his bruises. He even agreed to eat all the mangoes in his fruit bowl!

So don't worry, Momo the cheeky monkey did get better in...

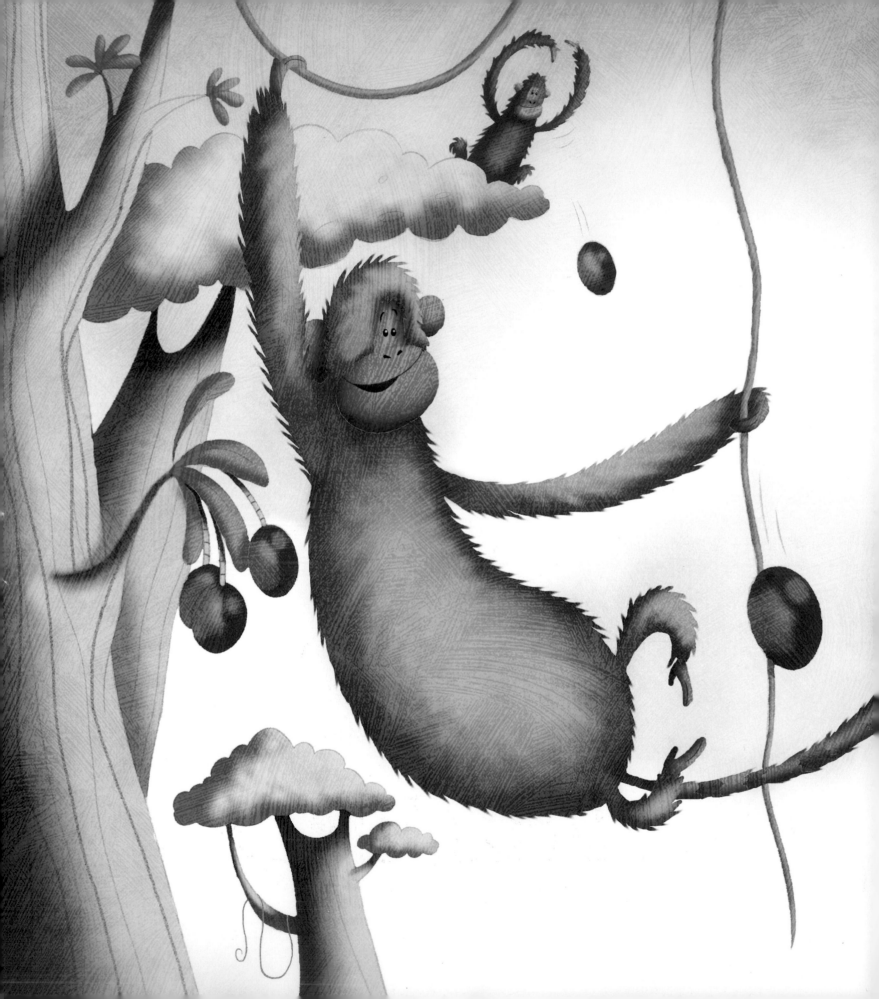

... THE END!

Emo the Elephant

Beyonce the Bear

Nurse Nibbles

George the
Giant Snail

Momo the Monkey

Giselle the Giraffe